First published by Parragon Books Ltd in 2015

Parragon Books Ltd
Chartist House
15–17 Trim Street
Bath BA1 1HA, UK
www.parragon.com

ISBN 978-1-4748-0837-8

Printed in China

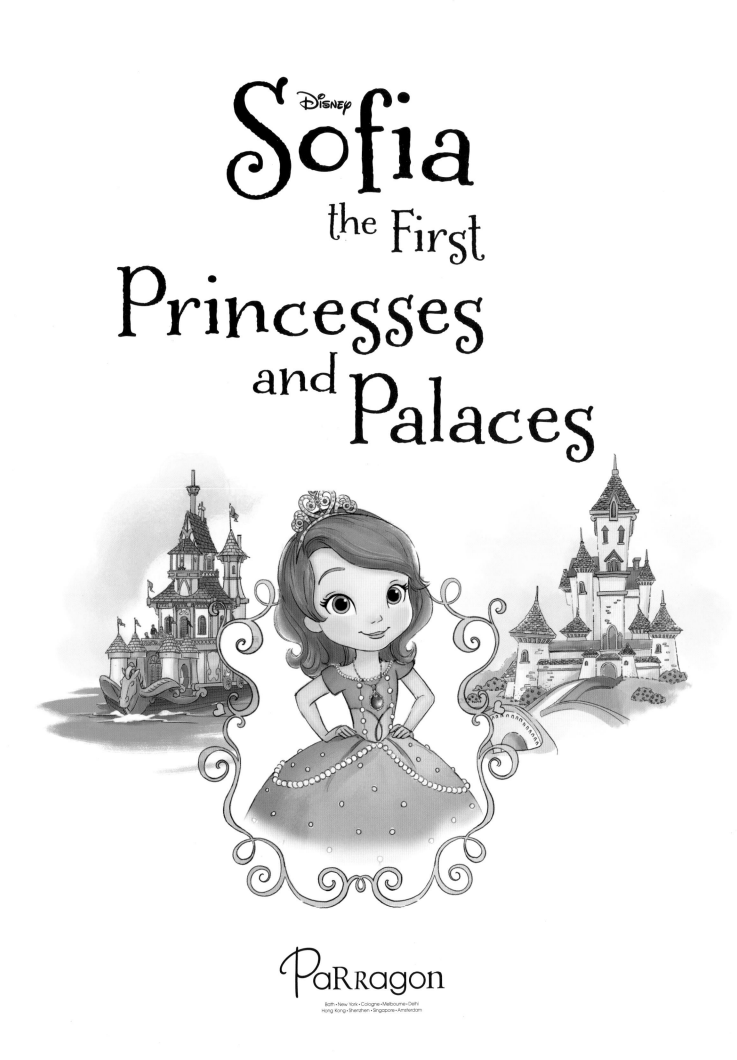

Disney
Sofia
the First
Princesses
and Palaces

PaRragon

Bath • New York • Cologne • Melbourne • Delhi
Hong Kong • Shenzhen • Singapore • Amsterdam

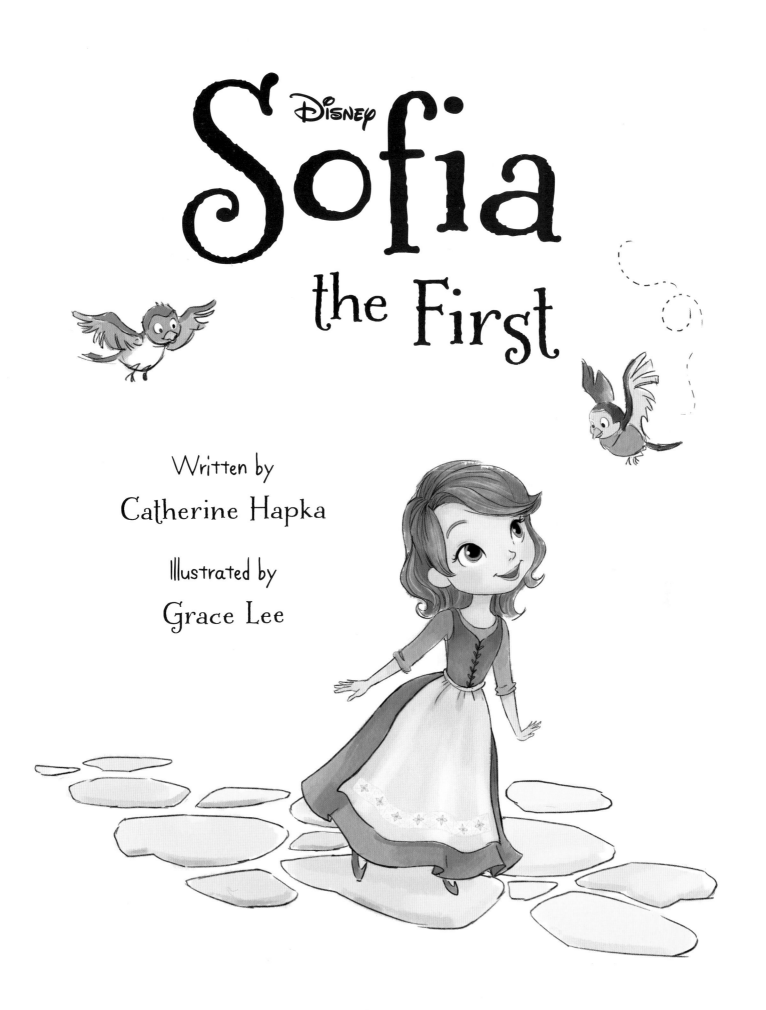

Disney Sofia the First

Written by
Catherine Hapka

Illustrated by
Grace Lee

My name is Sofia.

It used to be just me and my mum.
But then Mum married
King Roland. Now she's the
queen of Enchancia ...

... and I'm a
princess!

The trouble is, I don't really know anything about being a **princess**.

I've never had to do a royal wave ...

... I'm not sure when to curtsy ...

... or even which fork to use at dinner.

I'll never be as perfect a **princess** as my new stepsister, Amber.

"Just be yourself and you'll be fine,"
Mum tells me.

I'm not sure that will work. How can I be **myself** and be a princess at the same time?

Then King Roland – um,
I mean my new dad – tries to help.
He gives me a beautiful necklace
called the

Amulet of Avalor

Dad says it's a welcome-to-the-family gift
and that lots of **princesses** before me
have worn it.

Then he tells me we're having a royal ball in my honour. He says we'll dance the first waltz together. That's another thing I don't know how to do - dance!

Maybe there will be a dance class at my new school, Royal Prep Academy.

The headmistresses are three fairies named

Flora,

Fauna and

Merryweather.

They promise to
teach me everything
about being a
princess.

Hooray! I do have a dance class! Amber lends me a
pair of special shoes. I think she's starting to like me.

Oh, no!

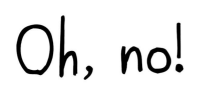

Amber tricked me!
These shoes are under
a **magic** spell.

The whole class laughs at me.
But even worse, I still don't know how to waltz,
and the **ball is tonight!**

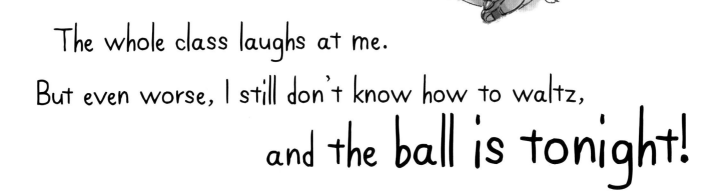

Then I remember Cedric, the sorcerer at the castle. James, my stepbrother, says he has all sorts of **magic** spells.

I ask Cedric to help. He writes down some **magic** words. He says if I read them out at the ball, I'll be able to waltz like a real **princess**.

"All hail Princess Sofia!"
says Baileywick as
I enter the ballroom.

"Shall we dance?"
the king asks.

I read out Cedric's **magic** words.

Somnibus

But I don't start to dance.

Populis Cella!

Instead, everyone at
the ball falls asleep –
even Cedric!

Oh, no!
What have I done? "Help!" I cry.

Suddenly,

my amulet

glows

and

Cinderella appears!

"Your amulet brought me here," she tells me. "When a **princess** is in trouble, another will come to help."

"Can you undo the spell, Cinderella?"
"No, I can't, but your new sister might be able to help."

"But Amber's been so mean to me!" I say.

Cinderella knows what it's like to
have mean stepsisters.
"I wish I had given my stepsisters
a second chance," she says.
"Perhaps that's what Amber needs."

Then she **disappears**.

Amber is still in her room. She never
made it to the ball. She finally tells me
why she's been acting so mean.

"I was worried that everyone would like
you more than me," she says sadly.

"No one could ever be as perfect a
princess as you, Amber!"

I tell her about Cedric's **magic** spell. We search his workshop ...

and find a spell that will wake everyone up.

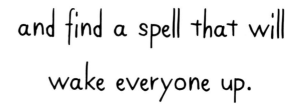

We hurry to the ballroom.

"Wait," Amber says. "I owe you a dance lesson."

Now I know we're true sisters – and **ever-after friends.**

When I get to the ballroom, I say the
magic words and everyone wakes up.
Then the king and I begin to waltz.

I look over at Amber and smile.
I can't believe how happy I am!
I think I'm going to fit into this
royal family after all.

"Sofia," my dad says, "I'm so proud of you. You dance wonderfully!"

"Thank you, Your Majesty – I mean, Dad."

"You know, Sofia, being a princess is about having a good heart. And you're going to make a great **princess**."

"Dad, I've been wondering ...
why do they call you King Roland the Second?"

"Because my father was also named Roland."

"Well ..." I say, "I guess that makes me

Sofia the First!"

And I am one princess who can't wait to see
what happens tomorrow and all the days
happily ever after!

Disney
Sofia
the First

The Floating Palace

Written by

Catherine Hapka

Illustrated by

Grace Lee

I'm Sofia

and I love being a ♥ princess.

For our summer holiday, my family is visiting Merroway Cove on our boat.

It's so big, it's more like a floating palace!

Lately, I've been reading about mermaids.
Maybe we'll see one at the cove. I hope so!
But Dad says mermaids aren't real.

My dad, King Roland, is usually right about most things – but he's wrong about mermaids.

Because when I go onto the deck of our floating palace, there she is – a real, live mermaid!

"Help!" the mermaid cries. Oh, no! She's tangled in a net!

"Let me help you," I say. I pull her onto
the boat and help to untangle her.
"Thank you!" she says. Her name is Oona.
She's really nice. Then she says she has to go.

"We're not supposed to spend time above the water,"
she explains. But when Oona gets in the water,
she can't swim. Her fin is hurt.

As I slide into the water to help her,
my amulet glows – and I turn into a

mermaid!

I can't believe it!
And neither can Oona.
"How did you do that?" Oona asks.
I tell her about my magical amulet.
Oona has a comb that's enchanted, too.
"I'm not sure what its powers are,"
says Oona, "but Mum says she'll
tell me when I'm older."

I help Oona swim towards her home in the cove. We swim past a kelp forest, a cool sunken ship and hundreds of beautiful fish.

When we get near Oona's home, I meet her friend, Sven the seahorse, and her big sister, Cora. They use moon kelp to heal Oona's tail.

Suddenly, the water goes dark.
It's our **floating palace**
stopping above us.

Then we hear Oona's mum
calling her and Cora home.
Oona's mum is the
mermaid queen.

"I'm so glad you're safe!"
she says. "A human vessel
is in the cove and humans
are dangerous."

I'm not dangerous and neither
is my family. Queen Emmaline
doesn't know that, though.

She wants to use
her magic trident to create
a powerful storm –
one that could blow the
floating palace out of the
cove, or maybe even sink it!
My family is on that ship!

So I tell the queen that
I'm a human and I can get the ship to leave.
"Please don't sink it. Just give me a chance," I say.
Luckily, the queen agrees to let me try.
Oona and Cora wish me luck.

I start swimming back to the floating palace.
Suddenly, I hear Oona calling my name.

Oh, no! A horrible, hideous sea monster
is chasing her! He wants her enchanted comb.
I swim after them as fast as I can,
but then they enter the kelp forest.

"Oona!" I cry.
There's no answer.

I rush back and tell
Queen Emmaline what happened.
She says I have till sundown
to rescue Oona.
The queen says if I can't,
she'll sink the floating palace!

I swim back to
the floating palace.
I need help, but my family
doesn't believe
in mermaids.

So I gather some friends who
do believe – Sven, Clover
and a seagull named Farley.

Finally, we find Oona. The sea monster
has her trapped and he's about to steal her
enchanted comb. I try to stop him, but he's very
powerful – he almost captures me, too!

Oh, no!

Queen Emmaline is starting loud thunder over the cove!

I need to rescue Oona before her mum sinks my family's ship.

I don't know what to do....

"Sofia, your necklace is glowing," Sven tells me.

When we dive underwater,
Princess Ariel appears!
My amulet brought her to help.
So I tell Ariel about Oona.
"I tried to save her, but...."
"You need more help," Ariel says.
She tells me that humans and
mermaids both love their families,
and if we just work together....

Now I know what to do!

Sven and I find
Cora and tell her
about the sea monster.

"He's after Oona's comb,"
I explain. "The only
way to save her is for
us to work together."

So Cora and
I come up with a plan.
Sven, Farley and Clover help, too.

I have to sneak onto the boat where the
sea monster has Oona trapped. I get there
just as he is about to cast a spell to grab
Oona's comb. I snatch it out of his hand!

"Give me the comb and I'll let your mermaid friend go," the sea monster says.

"What if I don't?" I say.

"Then I'll cast a spell on you and make you disappear!"

I step in front of Oona's cage.
Then I throw the comb
overboard, where Cora
is waiting to catch it.

"No you don't!"
the sea monster howls.
He flicks his wand at me ...

... but I quickly jump out
of the way. Instead of
making **me** disappear,
he makes Oona's cage vanish!

Oona is free! But the sea
monster is furious.
He points his wand at us.

"You won't trick me again!"
he warns.

Suddenly, Farley flies
over the sea monster –
and **drops** Clover right
on top of him!

Then Farley **swoops** down
and grabs his wand.

Cora holds up the comb
as it starts to glow!
"Waters, **rise** at my command!"
she cries. Then a spiral of water
blasts the sea monster
across the cove!

We rush back to Queen Emmaline.

"Thank goodness you're safe!" the queen cries.

She raises her trident to stop the storm.

Phew! Now my family is safe, too!

Oona's family and I go back to
the floating palace. We can't wait
for our two families to meet!
Dad admits he didn't think mermaids
were real, but now he knows!

I sit with Oona and watch the sun set.
She's a mermaid and I'm a human,
but I know
we'll be friends
forever!

Disney

Sofia
the First

Princesses
to the Rescue!

Adapted by
Catherine Hapka

Based on an episode by
Laurie Israel and
Rachel Ruderman

Illustrated by
Grace Lee

I'm Sofia

and being a princess is great!

My family gets to travel to lots of
interesting places, near and far.

Today we're visiting
the amazing **kingdom** of Wei-Ling.
Our friends Princess Jun and Prince Jin live here.

Soon after we arrive, James and Jin discover
a map to the **treasure** of the Jade Jaguar.
Before we know it, they're
running off to find it!

When we tell Jin's dad,
Emperor Quon,
where the boys went,
he looks worried.

"A **real** jaguar guards that treasure!" he exclaims. "We must stop them! Let's go!"

"We want to go with you and help," I say.

But the emperor says it's too dangerous for princesses.
Then he and my dad rush off.

I'm very worried, especially when the royal sorcerer
Wu-Chang tells us about the trap the jaguar set to protect
his treasure. Our brothers and fathers could become trapped!
Wu-Chang explains how to find the jaguar's cave.
He even tells us about a secret entrance!
"I will send for the guards to help," he says.
"But you must leave now."

We set out on the path, but soon we see some giant stone statues blocking our way.

Jun spots a sign that says 'The Maze of Warriors'. We try to enter the maze ... but a Stone warrior moves over and blocks us!

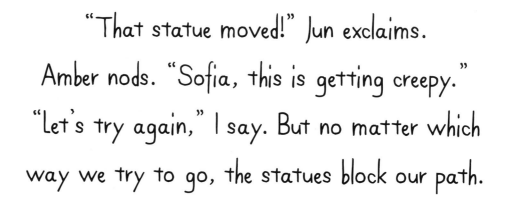

"That statue moved!" Jun exclaims.

Amber nods. "Sofia, this is getting creepy."

"Let's try again," I say. But no matter which
way we try to go, the statues block our path.

Amber and Jun are ready to give up.

"If we can't even make it past statues,

how are we going to get past a jaguar?" says Jun.

Maybe Amber and Jun are right.

Maybe we **should** turn back.

Then I notice my amulet.
It's **glowing!**

We turn round and
there's **Mulan!**
"Where do you think you're going?"
she asks us with a smile.
"I never gave up so easily. And neither should you.
You girls are stronger
than you know."

Mulan helps me climb on to a statue.
I leap to the next statue and the one after that.
Amber and Jun see they can do it, too,
and before we know it ...
"**We made it!**" Amber cries.

"See?" Mulan says.

"You girls are stronger than you thought."

"But we still have to save our families," I remind her.

"Can you help us, Mulan?"

"You have what it takes to get past anything

that comes your way," Mulan says. So we continue

along the path, but when I look back, Mulan is gone.

A little further down the path,
we hear a **buzzing** noise.
Suddenly, we're surrounded by moths.
There are so many that we can't
see where we're going!

"No way am I letting a bunch of
noisy bugs mess up my hair," Amber declares,
using her fan to shoo them away.

"Wow, Amber," I say.
"That was **amazing!**"
Amber twirls her fan.
"Now I'm ready to face
that jaguar," she says.

"I'm glad you're feeling braver,
Amber," I say. "We need all the
help we can get!"

Next the path leads to a lagoon
with huge scary-looking lizards
crouching on the shore.

"Lagoon Lizards," Jun explains.
"The meanest lizards in all of Wei-Ling!"

Amber tries to shoo the nearest lizard away with her fan, but it takes a **big** bite out of it!

"I **just** remembered something," Jun says, grabbing her flute. "Music calms them down." She begins to play a song.

Like magic,
the Lagoon Lizards stop snapping
their jaws and sway to the music.
I crouch beside one and whisper,
"Mr Lizard, could you take us across the lagoon?"
"We'd be happy to as long as
she keeps making music,"
the lizard replies.

I call to Amber and Jun.

"Look! These lizards are heading across. Let's hop on!"

It works!

Jun keeps playing music and the lizards carry us safely across the lagoon.

On the other side, there's a **waterfall**.
Then I spot something behind the wall of water: the
secret entrance to the cave Wu-Chang told us about!

We crawl through the
narrow tunnel entrance into the cave.
"Look at all the jewels!"
Amber exclaims.

We hear voices, so we follow them,
and we find everyone trapped in a deep pit.

"James! Dad!" I cry.
Dad looks amazed.
"You girls shouldn't be here,"
he says.

Suddenly, the Jade Jaguar leaps out
from behind his treasure!

ROAR!!!

Amber and Jun hide, but it's too late to turn back. We have to save our families. I have an idea! I grab a handful of jewels....

"You want these back?" I say to the jaguar. "Then catch me!"

I scramble back into the narrow tunnel and the jaguar
comes after me. "I'm stuck!" he roars.
"That was the plan," I say.

"I need you to let my friends and family go," I tell him.

"After they tried to take my treasure?" he asks.

I nod. "We don't want a single piece of your treasure.

We just want our families back."

The jaguar agrees to let them go,
so I ask Amber and Jun to help me get
him out of the tunnel. Then we find a rope
and help our families climb out of the pit.

Just as we're leaving the cave,
the guards Wu-Chang sent get there.
"You're too late," Amber says proudly.
Emperor Quon laughs. "Yes, the princesses already rescued us!"

Our dads didn't think we could do it, but they are so proud. And that night, there's a beautiful firework display – in honour of the three

bravest
rescuers
in the
land!

The End